D1411293

This book is dedicated to everyone
and everything involved
in its creation...

That includes the sun, the rain and the earth
for nourishing the trees which provided the paper
upon which to write and draw.

It includes all those who provided inspiration along the way.
It includes the printers, editors, publishers, distributors,
booksellers and anyone else who might have contributed,
in any big or small way, to the arrival of this book in your lap.

And lastly, it includes you, the reader, for reading it!

This book is one of a series of eight books from the "Now I Know..." series.

Each book is based upon one of the eight verses of mind training written by the 11th century Tibetan Buddhist master, Langri Thangpa.

Each verse, written in the back of the book, offers a different method for finding happiness, both for ourselves and for others too.

Now I Know...That I wouldn't be who I think I am, without other people.

Now I Know...That I'm not, actually, Mr. **Wonderful**.

Now I Know...That it's better to face my monsters.

Now I Know...That we all have a jewel inside us somewhere.

Now I Know...That I just have to look for the root and yank it out.

Now I Know...That silly hopes and fears will just make wrinkles on my face.

Now I Know...That it's better to keep quiet about the good things I do (and shout about the bad)

Now I Know...That I just have to keep my eye on the ball.

wishing to attain enlightenment
for the sake of all sentient beings,
who excel even the wish-fulfilling jewel,
May I constantly cherish them all.

Langri Thangpa (1054–1123)

A little bit extra at the end...

1. Look at the last page of the story. Try to explain why Esme is made up of blocks in this drawing. Which blocks would you say are the most important?

2. Make a drawing of yourself made up of blocks. Think about where you would put the most important blocks.

3. What did Esme learn from her Grandma? How did Esme's Grandma make sure she had Esme's attention before she began giving advice?

4. Do you know the names of any countries where it is not impolite to eat with your hands? Do you know of any other habits or customs that might mean different things in different countries?

5. Esme's Grandma tells her that without food she would be skinny. What does she say we need in order to eat? Can you think of other examples?

6. If you were alone in the world with no one to tell you how to eat, walk or talk, how do you think you would behave? Where would you live? What would you eat?

7. In what kind of ways do you think you might be different if you hadn't met your best friend? Your favourite pet? Your Grandma?

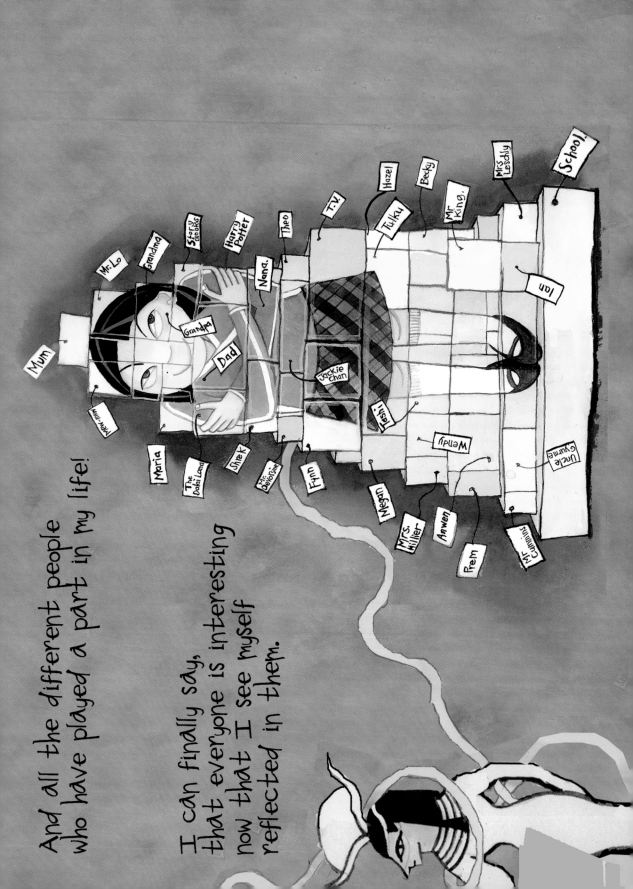

And all the different people who have played a part in my life!

I can finally say, that everyone is interesting now that I see myself reflected in them.

I tried to imagine she was just doing the weekly shopping run for her family and in her mind, my arm was simply her supermarket.

THE WILD ONES

You wouldn't know how to talk without other people!
You might be walking on your hands! Eating with your feet!
Sleeping in trees! We might all be wild things. Who knows?
We NEED other people, and THEY need US!

Night Night.
Esme.

"In fact, if there were no sheep or cotton plants or silkworms, not to mention textile factories, designers, tailors and clothes shops, you would be sitting there, on that rough, bushy ground.... Naked!

And if there were no food factories or supermarkets with all their shelf stackers and cashiers and managers, then your mum would be unable to feed you and you would be both naked and skinny! Helpless, unschooled, unable to do anything!

And finally, if we were to take away your mother and father — the two people who created you — there would be no YOU at all!"

"Without the hard work of ALL these people, your bottoms would not be sitting, as they do every day, on those chairs in that school. In fact, those chairs would not be on that carpet, that carpet would not be on that concrete floor, that concrete floor would not have been laid on those foundations, those foundations would not have been dug deep into the land and the land would be all rough and bushy and full of trees."

Painters and plasterers finished the job. Then gardeners, computer technicians, cooks, caretakers and cleaners were hired. Finally, when everything looked ready, teachers and pupils arrived."

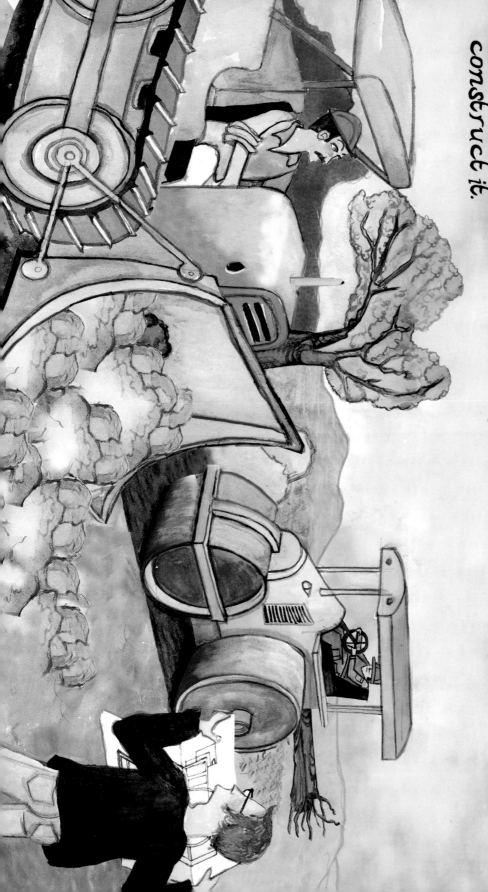

"Then there's your school. In order to build your school, someone had to have a plan, then land had to be bought, cleared and leveled... Architects had to design the building, then builders, plumbers, electricians, carpenters and glaziers worked together to construct it.

Director — Anwen Rabsel Drolma
Focus Puller — Ian Alexander Bell
Production Runner — Frank Wahrheit
Set supervisor — Frank Gridley
Dialogue Editor — Frances McDonald
Best Boy — Yann Devorsine
Script Writer — Beth Williams
Costume Assistant — Dechen Leschly
Graphic Designer — Mirese Van der Vliet
Catering — SIMMONDS
Painter — Charlotte Davies
Riggers — Anya and Hiram
Props Master — William James Day
Choreography — Shana Devje
Set Decorators — George and Lily
Personal Assistant — Ruby King
Gaffer — Noha Ecenarro
Continuity — Adrien
Stills Photographer — Graham Hazlehurst
Team Coordinator — Lucy Needham
Dubbing Mixer — George Pierce
Special Effects — Emma, Laura and David
Stuntmen — Marley and Tom Becam
Music — Tom Devje

"And?" asked Grandma

"And Costume Designers, and Photographers and Hairdressers..."

"And?"

"And Stuntmen and Gaffers and Best Boys and all those other funny names you see at the end of a film..."

"A ha!" said Grandma.

"So, how were those movies made?"

"with camera men?"

"Erm, with actors and actresses?"

"Sound Technicians?"

"Directors and Scriptwriters?"

"Personal Assistants?"

"Make-up artists?"

"But why would he feel shy?" asked Grandma.

"Because of everyone else, because they'd all be staring and laughing at him."

"Exactly!" said Grandma.
"Now, why does your friend Ryder wear clothes, even when it's very, very hot outside?"

"Because otherwise he would be naked of course! He'd feel shy!"

"I suppose it's because that's what everyone else does in this country... If he ate with his hands, other people might think he was rude?"

"Let's talk about Theo.
from nextdoor."

Said Grandma.

"Why does he eat with
a knife and fork?"

"I suppose it's because
his Mum tells him to,
like mine does.
My Mum says it's polite."

"Why?"

Asked Grandma.

"And, as you grow and become your own little person, her love grows too...

All the things she thought were important before, are pushed aside...

She sells her piano to buy you a bicycle

she gives up her French classes so you can learn Karate.

All your mother's thoughts are now just for you.

Everything about you is beautiful to her.
From the scent of your soft,
baby hair, to the
smelly, dirty
nappies
she is
constantly
changing
for you.

Her life is
completely
yours now."

"Then, on the day of the birth,
the mother experiences
the most incredible pain...
Like no pain she's ever felt before.

Some say it's like all the pain
she's ever felt before
rolled into one...

(and times by 10)

But she doesn't complain
because she knows that
when the pain is over,
you will be there,
a new baby,
the object of her love."

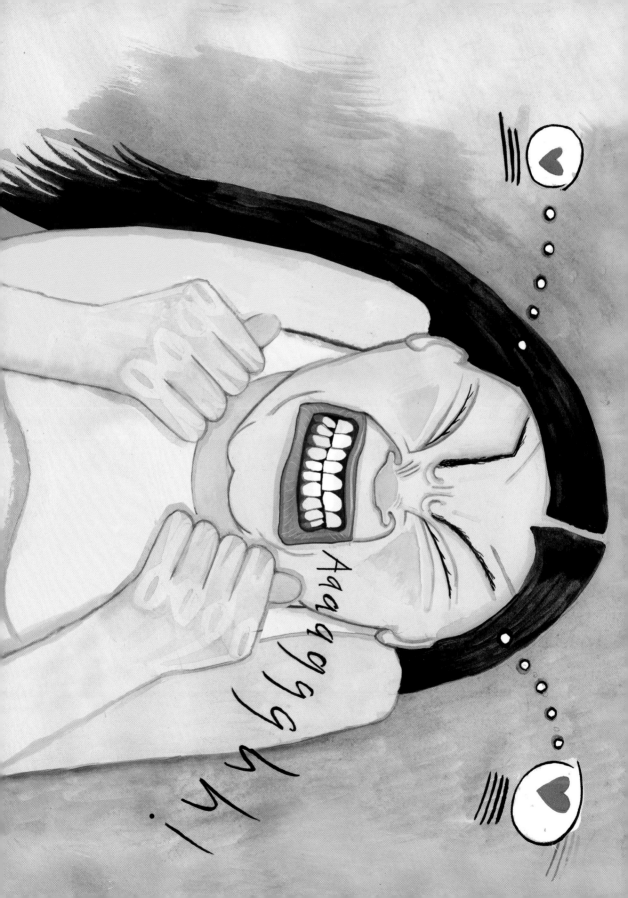

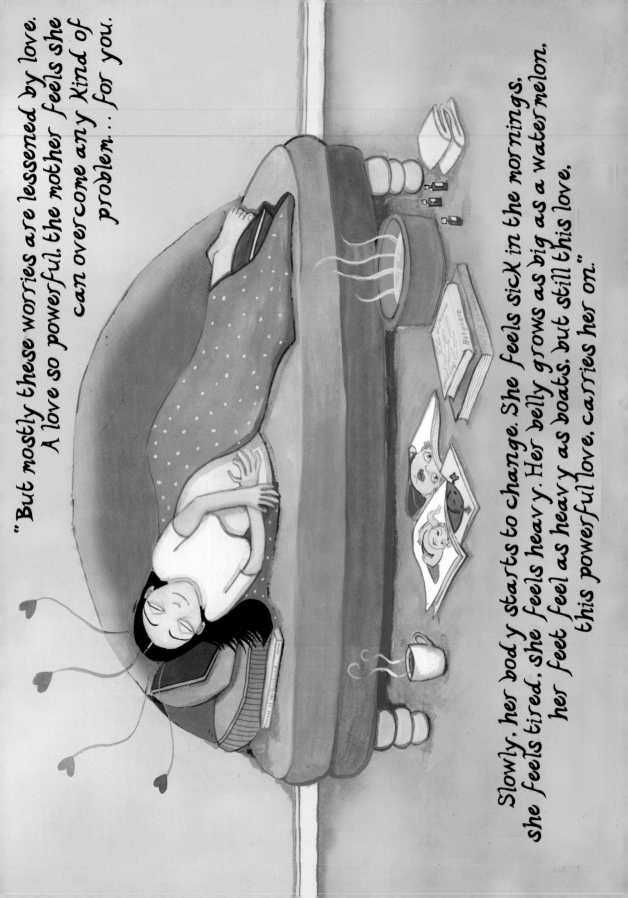

"But mostly these worries are lessened by love. A love so powerful the mother feels she can overcome any kind of problem... for you.

Slowly, her body starts to change. She feels sick in the mornings, she feels tired, she feels heavy. Her belly grows as big as a watermelon, her feet feel as heavy as boats, but still this love, this powerful love, carries her on."

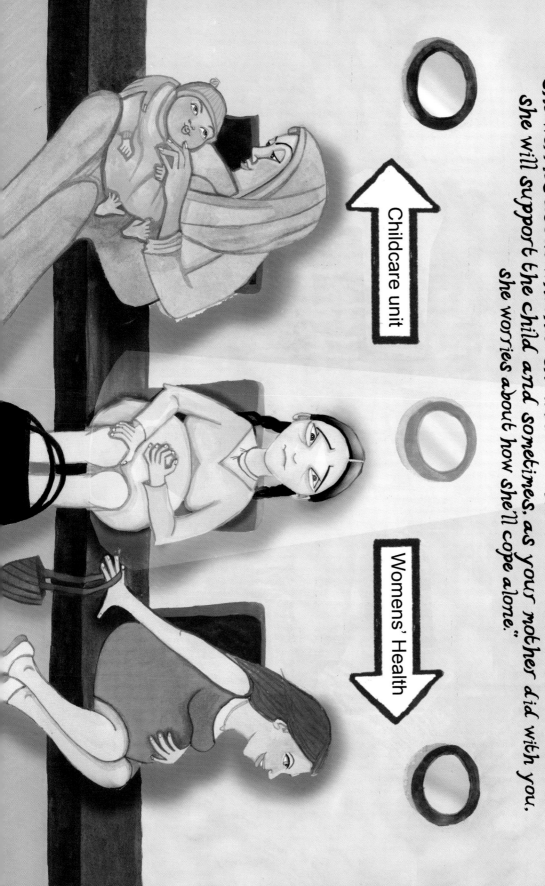

"Now, let me tell you a few realities. When a woman finds out she is going to have a baby, she worries. She worries about whether she will make a good mother, she worries about whether she'll know what to do, she worries about how she will support the child and sometimes, as your mother did with you, she worries about how she'll cope alone."

Childcare unit

Womens' Health

"OK" said Grandma
"Shall I start?"

"But first," said Grandma,

"I want you to make a picture in your mind of what your life might be like if your Mum wasn't around."

"Don't say anything to me, just make the picture..."

But then, my Grandma came to live with us.

She seemed a bit shocked by my attitude.

On her third night, she sat me down and we had a little chat

I had no friends, and I didn't really want any either...

I thought I was the most important person in the whole world and everyone else was just put there to keep me happy.

NOW I KNOW...

that I wouldn't be who I think I am,

without other people.

by Sally Devorsine

THE DALAI LAMA

ENDORSEMENT

Geshe Langri Thangpa (1054–1123 CE) was a Buddhist master famous in Tibet for his 'Eight Verses of Mind Training'. He originally wrote them down for his own personal use, but they have later become an invaluable guide for many other practitioners down the centuries. The proof of their worth is that these practical instructions on how to make oneself and others happy in everyday situations are just as relevant today, for both adults and children, as they were nearly 1,000 years ago. This I can say from my own experience, for I myself was introduced to them when I was a young boy and I have recited them every day since then. When I meet with difficult circumstances, I reflect on their meaning and I find it helpful.

Sally Devorsine teaches English in Bhutan to the young reincarnation of a lama who was one of my own esteemed teachers, Dilgo Khyentse Rinpoche. She was inspired by the verses of Langri Thangpa to create these colourful storybooks, initially to entertain her young student. Later, she realised that they might provide a way to introduce some of the longstanding values that we Tibetans hold dear to children elsewhere in the world today.

If we are to ensure a peaceful future for our world, I believe that it is important that we foster positive values like compassion, kindness and love in our children's minds from an early age. Certainly books like these can help us do that. Each of these stories shows the young reader a different way to secure happiness, whether it is by recognising anger when it arises, being aware of how our every action has an effect on others, or looking beyond our first impressions of people we meet.

I congratulate Sally Devorsine on her efforts and hope that these charming books have the edifying result she intended. I am sure they will delight readers young and old.

March 25, 2011